GROVER'S BAD, AWFUL DAY

SESAME STREET
A GROWING-UP BOOK™

By Anna H. Dickson / Illustrated by Tom Brannon

A SESAME STREET / GOLDEN PRESS BOOK
Published by Western Publishing Company, Inc. in conjunction with Children's Television Workshop.

2325843

One morning Grover slept late.
"Oh, my goodness!" he said, jumping out of bed.
"I will be late to play group!"
As he ran to the bathroom, he stubbed his furry toe.
"Ouch!" he said. "That smarts!"

R405326

Grover squeezed toothpaste onto his toothbrush, but it fell off before it got to his mouth. Then he bumped the toothpaste cap off the edge of the sink, and it bounced down the drain.

Then he combed his fur, and
the comb caught in the tangles.
The more he pulled, the more it
hurt.

"Oh, dear," said Grover.

At breakfast, Grover poured milk on the table instead
of on his Monsterberry Crunch.

"Take your time, dear," said his mommy.

So he did, and he wasn't ready when Herry came to
walk with him to play group.

Mommy kissed him. "Good-by, my little Grover. Do not forget your lunch," she called as she rushed off to work. "And wear your rubber boots. It is going to rain!"

"Oh, no," Grover said to Herry. "I do not want to wear my rubber boots. They go *galumph galumph* when I walk. And I do not want it to rain!"

Grover and Herry were late to play group.
Show-and-Tell had already started. They had to walk
in front of everybody to find a place to sit.
"Oh, I am so embarrassed!" thought Grover.

During Art, Grover made a picture of Barkley, but he
drew his head too big. He tried again, but this time he
drew his legs too long. He drew Barkley again and
colored him, but when he cut out the picture he cut off
Barkley's tail by mistake.

Grover tore up the picture.

"It did not look like Barkley anyway," he said.

During Alphabet, Grover forgot what comes after Q.
"Grover," said Miss Tighe, "you are having a bad day."

During Music, he tried to honk his nose like the
Honkers, but it didn't make a noise!
"Try *blowing* it, Fur Face! Heh, heh," said Oscar.

In the park at playtime, Grover saw the Mighty
Monsters playing tackle football.

"Oh, may I please play, too?" he asked. "Please may I?"

"You're too little," said Monty, the biggest monster,
and the other monsters laughed.

"I did not want to play football anyway,"
Grover grumbled.

At lunchtime, Grover reached into his cubby for his cute little lunchbox, but it was not there.

"Oh, no!" cried Grover. "I forgot my lunch."

"Don't worry, Grover," said Betty Lou. "My mom always makes me an extra sandwich in case I'm extra hungry. You may have it."

"But I like peanut-butter-and-jelly," he wailed.

"That's what I have," said Betty Lou.

"Terrific!" said Grover. "Thank you, Betty Lou."

But when Grover took a bite, he made a face. "Yucch!" he whispered to Herry. "Betty Lou's mommy puts strawberry jelly in her sandwiches. My mommy always gives me grape. Strawberry has seeds!"

"Grover," said Herry, "you are having a bad day."

"I am having a bad, *awful* day!" said Grover.

After play group, Grover and Herry stopped at the ice-cream truck. Grover ordered a grape ice-cream cone. He took such a big first bite that he knocked the ice cream right out of the cone, *plop*, onto the sidewalk.

And then it started to rain.

"I knew it!" cried Grover. "I am having a bad, awful day!"

So, *galumph galumph*, Grover and Herry ran home in
the rain. They ran until, suddenly, Grover stopped.

"Herry!" he said. "I cannot move. My rubber boot that
my mommy made me wear because of the rain is stuck to
the sidewalk!"

"You must have stepped in some gum, Grover," said Herry.

Every time Grover put down his boot, it stuck to the sidewalk again. And every time his boot stuck, Grover got madder.

"This is ridiculous!" he yelled. "MOMMIEEE!"

Grover left his boot stuck to the sidewalk and stomped home in one boot.

"I had a bad, awful day!" Grover told his mommy as
soon as he got home. "I was late to play group, and the
big monsters wouldn't let me play with them, and I
forgot that R comes after Q. My nose wouldn't honk in
Music, and my ice cream fell on the sidewalk, and now
it is raining!"

"Where is your other boot, Grover?" his mommy asked.

Grover sat in his mommy's lap and told her
everything. Then he began to cry. "My bad, awful day
made me feel bad and awful."

She gave him a hug. "Bad days happen to everyone,"
she said. "When one happens to you, just keep doing
your best. And never let a bad day make you feel bad
about yourself!"

She rubbed his furry head dry with a towel.

"Come on, dear. Let's go get your boot."

Grover and his mommy walked back to get his boot. Mommy unstuck it and cleaned off the gum. She poured out the water and dried it inside so Grover could put it on again.

Then Mommy took Grover to Hooper's Store and ordered two grape ice-cream sodas. Grover's friends were there.

"Hey, Grover," Monty Monster called to him. "Tomorrow we're going to play tickle football instead of tackle football. It's not dangerous. You want to play?"

"Oh, sure, Monty! I will be there!" said Grover.

"I think tomorrow will be a better day."